D0618448

Copyright © 2010 by NordSüd Verlag AG, CH-8005 Zürich, Switzerland.
First published in Switzerland under the title *Der Fuchs, die Hühner und das Wurstbrot*.
English translation copyright © 2010 by North-South Books Inc., New York 10001.
All rights reserved.
No part of this book may be reproduced or utilized in any form or by any means,
electronic or mechanical, including photo-copying, recording, or any information storage
and retrieval system, without permission in writing from the publisher.

First published in the United States, Great Britain, Canada, Australia, and New Zealand
in 2010 by North-South Books Inc., an imprint of NordSüd Verlag AG, CH-8005 Zürich, Switzerland.
Distributed in the United States by North-South Books Inc., New York 10001.

Library of Congress Cataloging-in-Publication Data is available.
ISBN: 978-0-7358-2295-5 (trade edition)
Printed in Belgium by Proost N.V., B 2300 Turnhout, November 2009.
1 3 5 7 9 • 10 8 6 4 2

www.northsouth.com

FSC
Mixed Sources
Product group from well-managed
forests and other controlled sources

Cert no. BV-COC-070303
www.fsc.org
© 1996 Forest Stewardship Council

Friederike Rave

Outfoxing the Fox

NorthSouth
New York / London

TETON COUNTY LIBRARY
JACKSON, WYOMING

Once there was a little fox who liked to stay in bed late. He didn't feel like going to school. "I'm a fox, after all," he thought. "And foxes are clever enough already."

At breakfast, he dreamed up an idea for
dinner: chicken fricassee! "I'll go visit the hens,"
he said. But what if the hunter was out hunting
and tried to shoot him?

"I'll go at night," said the fox, "when the hunter
can't see me. People can't see in the dark. But
foxes can see in the dark very well. Every crafty
fox knows that."

So that night, the fox set off for the henhouse.

"Anybody home?" called the fox. "Mmmmm. It smells like nice plump hens in here."

"It smells like *fox* in here," said the rooster. "What do you want, Foxy?"

"Well," said the fox, "I'd like a nice chicken fricassee for dinner. I thought maybe you could help me out."

The hens said nothing. They just clucked quietly to one another until the fox grew impatient.

"Can I have a chicken or not?" he demanded.

"Come in and have a seat," said
the hens. "Let's talk this over."
The fox nodded politely and
climbed up onto the roost.

But when he got close to the hens, the fox had
a shock. These hens didn't look like the hens in
his cookbook. These hens looked sick!

"Are you all right?" he asked.

"We've all caught terrible colds," said the hens,
and they sniffled and sneezed all over the fox.

"One of us would love to be a delicious chicken
fricassee for you," said a hen, "but as you can
see—*COUGH COUGH*—we're not feeling very tasty
at the moment."

"You are obviously a very crafty fox, and no doubt a fine cook," said another. "You're too smart to want to catch a cold. Wait a little while. We'll let you know when we're feeling better."

"Okay," said the fox. Then, waving good-bye, he hastily left the henhouse and went home to bed.

Every night the fox went to visit the hens. And every night they said the same thing.

"We're sorry, dear fox, but we're still feeling under the weather."

The fox was beginning to get angry. "There's something not quite right here," he muttered. "I think these hens are trying to pull the wool over my eyes."

Monday   **Tuesday**   **Wednesday**

Thursday   **Friday**

On Friday, the fox went home in a very bad
mood. Worse still, he had spent so much time
with the hens, he was beginning to think he was
getting sick himself.

"I think I may have caught a cold," he moaned.
"And I'm still hungry!"

That night he dreamed of rabbit stew.

The next morning, the fox crept outside. He felt so weak, he could hardly move. He was so slow, the rabbits and mice, and even the snails, all laughed at him.

"I'm hungry," the fox groaned as he shuffled across the field.

Suddenly, the fox came upon a sleeping hunter. And right next to the hunter was a big, juicy sausage sandwich!

"I wouldn't mind that at all," thought the fox, and he crept over to the sandwich. But on the way, his bushy tail swept over the hunter's nose. The hunter woke with a start and began to sneeze.

He sneezed so hard, his glasses fell off. "Just you wait, you cheeky fox!" he shouted. But without his glasses, he couldn't find his gun.

The fox grabbed the sausage sandwich and ran for his life.

The fox curled up in bed with his sandwich. Mmmmm. He began to feel better.

"I'm such a crafty fox," he thought. "I really tricked that hunter. In fact, I'm so crafty, I'm going to trick those chickens too. I think I just might pay them another visit tomorrow night."

As for the chickens, they weren't waiting around.